Lester's Dreadful Sweaters

Kids Can Press acknowledges the financial support of the Government of Ontario, through the Ontario Media Development Corporation's Ontario Book Initiative; the Ontario Arts Council; the Canada Council for the Arts; and the Government of Canada, through the BPIDP, for our publishing activity.

Published in Canada by
Kids Can Press Ltd.
25 Dockside Drive
Toronto, ON M5A 0B5

Published in the U.S. by
Kids Can Press Ltd.
2250 Military Road
Tonawanda, NY 14150

www.kidscanpress.com

Kids Can Press is a *Corus*™ Entertainment company

The artwork in this book was rendered in pencil crayon.
The text is set in Bookeyed Jack.

Edited by Tara Walker and Yvette Ghione
Designed by Karen Powers

This book is smyth sewn casebound.
Manufactured in Tseung Kwan O, NT Hong Kong, China, in 5/2012 by Paramount Printing Co. Ltd.

CM 12 0 9 8 7 6 5 4 3 2 1

Library and Archives Canada Cataloguing in Publication

Campbell, K.G.
Lester's dreadful sweaters / written and illustrated by K.G. Campbell.

ISBN 978-1-55453-770-9

I. Title.

PZ7.C15512Les 2012   j813'.6   C2011-908296-9

*For Ricky and Louie,
without whom none
of this would have
been possible*

Lester's Dreadful Sweaters

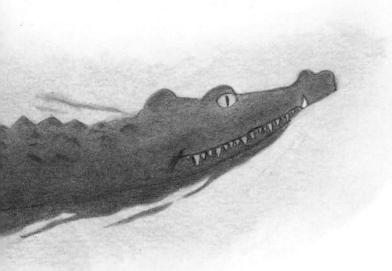

Written and illustrated by
K.G. CAMPBELL

KIDS CAN PRESS

COUSIN CLARA'S cottage was consumed by a crocodile.
Luckily, Cousin Clara wasn't in it.

Upon hearing the news, Lester disapproved.
"Cottages," he muttered, "aren't meant for munching."

He added crocodiles to his list of Suspicious Stuff Starting with C.

Then he checked that his socks were even ...

... and combed his hair.

No one knew exactly whose cousin Cousin Clara was,
so she came to stay with Lester's family.
She was little and frilly and came with a basket of knitting.
"I added crocodiles to my list," Lester assured her.

At first, everything went well enough. Clara didn't make unsavory noises or rearrange Lester's Lost and Found collection. All she did was sit and knit, clickety-click, clickety-click.

One morning, she said, "I made you a sweater." And Lester thought, "How kind ..."

... until he saw it.

It was shriveled yet saggy.
It had holes where it shouldn't
and none where it should.
It was a less-than-pleasant yellow
and smothered with purple pom-poms.

It was DREADFUL.

"Say thank you, Lester," said Lester's mother.

"Thank you," whispered Lester.

"He'll wear it to school," said Lester's father.

Lester's day did not go well.

Mr. Twist didn't compliment his carefully combed hair (which he ALWAYS did). And Enid Measles made a less-than-pleasant remark.

Later, Lester's sweater was discovered in the laundry,
all stringy and shrunken.
"What a mysterious accident," said Lester.
"Not to worry," said Cousin Clara.
And she kept on knitting, clickety-click, clickety-click.

The next morning, there was another sweater. This one covered bits it shouldn't and didn't cover bits it should. It was an irksome pink and dotted with oddly placed upside-down pockets.

It was GHASTLY.

"Don't you look handsome," said Lester's mother as she handed him his lunch.

Lester's day went worse than the one before.
Mr. Twist didn't notice his nicely knotted tie
(which he ALWAYS did). And Enid Measles
said several irksome things.

Later, Lester's sweater was discovered in the yard,
shredded by the lawn mower.
"It's an inexplicable tragedy," said Lester.
"Never mind," said Cousin Clara.
And still she knitted, clickety-click, clickety-click.

The next sweater was
repulsively pumpkin,
uncommonly crooked and
had a hideous hood.
IT unraveled in the
rain and got washed
down a drain.

The next was an awful
olive and had alarmingly
large buttons. IT was
pecked to pieces by several
outraged ostriches.

Then there was the terribly turquoise one with several unexpected sleeves. IT got stolen by ne'er-do-wells.

It seemed that as fast as she could knit them, Cousin Clara's creations were doomed to disaster.

"I have curiously bad luck with sweaters," Lester explained.
"Luckily," said Cousin Clara, "I'm a curiously speedy knitter."

That night, long after bedtime, Lester could hear a frantic
clickety-clickety-clickety-click.

At dawn, he arose to a bone-chilling sight.
In the parlor loomed a woolly MOUNTAIN
of cruel colors, appalling polka dots,
frightening stripes, startling tassels and
things with six fingers.

"OH, NO!" wailed Lester. "Enid Measles' party is today!"

They found him crouched amidst the remains
of grimly dismembered garments. He clutched
a large pair of scissors, and his hands were
covered with red yarn.

Lester's parents said some loud and angry stuff.
Lester said he was sorry.
Cousin Clara didn't say anything.
She just smiled and held up ...

ANOTHER sweater.

When Lester arrived at Enid's, Mrs. Measles said,
"You must be with the clowns."
"I'm doomed," Lester explained, "to a life of
dreadful sweaters."

Lester disapproved of clowns.

"Noses," he mumbled, "are not for honking."

But the clowns liked Lester. "We love your sweater,"
they told him.
"You don't think," gasped Lester, "it's dreadful?"
"The feathers and feet," said the clowns, "are super cute."

"Would you," asked Lester hopefully, "like your OWN?"

"There are more?" shrieked the clowns.

"By now," said Lester, "there should be tons. Follow me."

On seeing Cousin Clara's freshly knitted collection,
the clowns went nuts.
"So stylish," they cried, "so fresh, so inspired!"
"Oh, STOP," giggled Cousin Clara, knitting away,
clickety-click.

"We'll take them all!" declared the head clown.
"Can you make more?"
"Cousin Clara," Lester assured him, "is a curiously
speedy knitter."
On the spot, Cousin Clara was offered a job,
knitting for the whole troupe.

"Does your act," asked Cousin Clara,
"involve crocodiles?"

It didn't. But the position
DID include a fanciful caravan
of Clara's very own. So she accepted
the offer and packed up her knitting.

"Won't you," asked the clowns, "miss your family?"
"I'm not sure," said Cousin Clara, "if we're even related."

After everyone was gone, Lester discovered
a honking nose and a left-behind sweater.
It was a gruesome hue of maroon and had
itchy, ill-fitting bits with bells.
Lester eyed the garbage can.

But then he carefully cataloged both things and added them to the Lost and Found.

"Just in case," he murmured, "I ever become a clown."

THE END